ALL
ABOARD
READING™
Level 2
Grades 1-3

HELLO, Two-Wheeler!

By Jane B. Mason
Illustrated by David Monteith

Grosset & Dunlap • New York

It is summer.

And it is hot.

I am hanging around
with my dog Fred.

Put Beginning Readers on the Right Track with
ALL ABOARD READING™

The All Aboard Reading series is especially for beginning readers. Written by noted authors and illustrated in full color, these are books that children really and truly *want* to read—books to excite their imagination, tickle their funny bone, expand their interests, and support their feelings. With three different reading levels, All Aboard Reading lets you choose which books are most appropriate for your children and their growing abilities.

Level 1—for Preschool through First Grade Children
Level 1 books have very few lines per page, very large type, easy words, lots of repetition, and pictures with visual "cues" to help children figure out the words on the page.

Level 2—for First Grade to Third Grade Children
Level 2 books are printed in slightly smaller type than Level 1 books. The stories are more complex, but there is still lots of repetition in the text and many pictures. The sentences are quite simple and are broken up into short lines to make reading easier.

Level 3—for Second Grade through Third Grade Children
Level 3 books have considerably longer texts, use harder words and more complicated sentences.

All Aboard for happy reading!

For Jared and Caitlin—J.B.M.

For Barb, who believed—D.M.

Text copyright © 1995 by Jane B. Mason. Illustrations copyright © 1995 by David Monteith. All rights reserved. Published by Grosset & Dunlap, Inc., which is a member of The Putnam & Grosset Group, New York. ALL ABOARD READING is a trademark of The Putnam & Grosset Group. GROSSET & DUNLAP is a trademark of Grosset & Dunlap, Inc. Published simultaneously in Canada. Printed in the U.S.A.

Library of Congress Cataloging-in-Publication Data

Mason, Jane.
  Hello, two-wheeler! / by Jane Mason ; illustrated by David Monteith.
     p.   cm.—(All aboard reading)
  Summary: Even though he loves to ride his bicycle, a young boy makes excuses not to because he is the only one of his friends to still have training wheels.
  [1. Bicycles and bicycling—Fiction.]   I. Monteith, David,
ill. II. Title. III. Series.
PZ7.M4116He   1995
[E]—dc20
                                                         94-28633
                                                         CIP
                                                         AC

ISBN 0-448-40854-6 (GB)   A B C D E F G H I J
ISBN 0-448-40853-8 (pbk.)   A B C D E F G H I J

Outside all the kids zoom
up and down the street
on their two-wheelers.
They yell and have fun.

"Why don't you get
your bike out too?"
my mom asks.

"No," I say.

"I want to play with Fred."

But that is not really true.

I do not want the kids

to see my training wheels.

I used to love riding my bike
with all the kids.
I liked the feel of the wind.
I liked the blur of the trees.
I liked tooting my bike horn.

But now everybody can ride
without training wheels.
Everybody but you-know-who!

Every night Dad tries to help me.

We go to a big parking lot.

We take off the training wheels.

"Okay," Dad says.

"I will hold on to you.

You just pedal."

So I do.

But then Dad says,

"I am letting go now."

And I get scared.

I think about falling.

My feet won't stay

on the pedals.

And I stop.

It happens every time.

"You can do it,"

Dad keeps saying.

"Just don't think about it."

But how do I do that?

We always end up going home
with my training wheels
back on my bike.

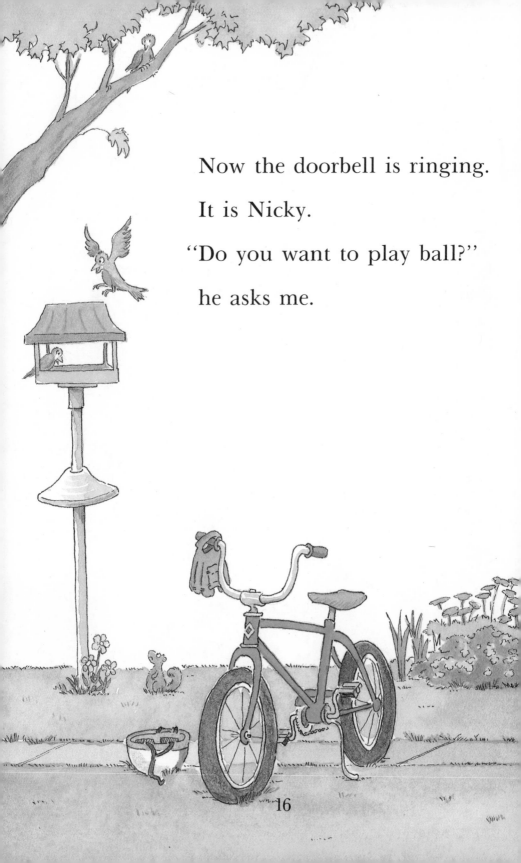

Now the doorbell is ringing.

It is Nicky.

"Do you want to play ball?"

he asks me.

The ball field is far away.
You have to ride your
bike there.
"Sorry," I tell him.
"I have to
clean my room."

Later the phone rings.

It is Nate.

"Want to bike down

the big hill?" he asks me.

I think fast.

I fake a sneeze.

ACHOO!

"I can't," I say.

"I have a cold."

Then we hang up.

I am bored.

So I go over to see Tommy.

Tommy lives next door.

At Tommy's house

there are lots of things to do—

without riding a bike.

We work on a model plane.

We play video games.

We shoot hoops.

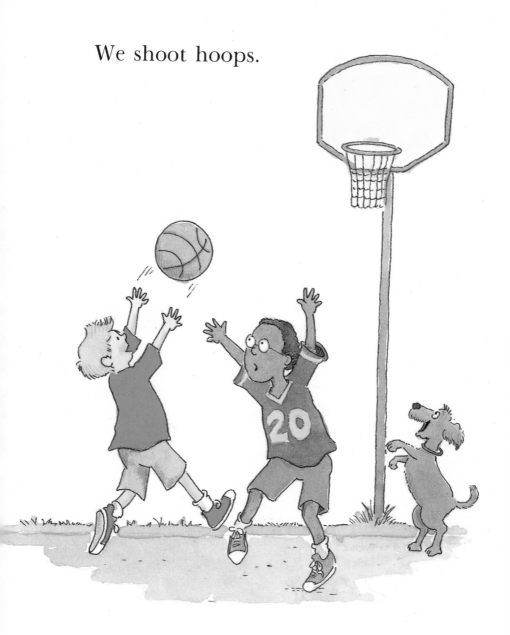

I am having fun.

Who cares about two-wheelers?

But then our friend Josh
rides by.
"A bunch of kids are going
swimming at the pond.
Want to come?"

Tommy's eyes light up.

But mine do not.

What can I say this time?

"Um. I—I have to wash my dog.
There is a big dog show
coming up."

"It's not until next week,"
Josh says.

"I know." I try to sound cool.

"But I want to get Fred
super clean."

Tommy comes over to me.

"Come on," he says.

"No one will care about
your training wheels."

Tommy is the only one
who knows my secret.

I shake my head.

"You go. Maybe I'll come later."

25

At home

I flop on the couch.

Fred _is_ kind of smelly.

But I do not want

to give him a bath.

I want to be with my friends

at the pond.

Then I get an idea.

A good idea!

I put on my swim trunks.

I get Dad's tools.

"I am going to the pond,"

I tell my mom.

I hop on my bike and go.

It feels so good to ride!

I like the wind in my face.

I like the blur of the trees.

I like tooting my bike horn.

Soon I am near the pond.

I stop.

I take off my training wheels

and hide them.

Then I walk my bike over

to the kids.

"Hi!" says Tommy.

He looks surprised and happy.

"I'm glad you came."

The kids are swimming.

I jump in.

"Don't you have a cold?"

Nate says.

I say, "It went away.

It must have been

the two-hour kind."

"Did you get Fred washed?"

Josh asks.

I shake my head.

"Nope. We were out of

dog shampoo."

Then somebody starts a water fight.

Nobody asks me anything else.

We have a great time.

But then it is time to go.

We all get on our bikes.

"Oh! Something is not right

with my pedal," I say.

"Lucky for me I have my tools.

You guys go on.

I will catch up."

Tommy gives me a funny look.

But he rides off with the kids.

I walk my bike to the bushes.

I put my training wheels back on.

Then I get on my bike and go.

Nobody will see me now.

They are too far ahead.

I ride past the pond.

I ride down the hill.

I make a turn.

Oh, no! Up ahead

I see all the kids.

Tommy starts shouting.

He is pointing at my wheels.

Oh, no! Oh, no!

Everyone will see.

"Way to go!" Tommy shouts.

What is he talking about?

I look down.

Yikes!

No training wheels.

I keep going.

I am too scared to stop.

I do what Dad says.

I try not to think about it.

I just keep riding.

"See you!" I shout

to the kids.

And do you know what?

I make it all the way home.

Good-bye, training wheels!

Hello, two-wheeler!